Sing a Song of Sixpence

Sing a song of sixpence,
A pocket full of rye.
Four and twenty blackbirds
Baked in a pie.
When the pie was opened,
The birds began to sing.
Oh, wasn't that a dainty dish
to set before the king?

adapted by Jeffrey B. Fuerst
illustrated by Lon Levin

The baker rises early on baking day.
The baker has many things to make.
First, he makes cookies for the prince.

Next, he makes muffins for the princess. Then, he makes a cake for the queen. Last, he makes a pie for the king.

"My cookies will be sweet!"
said the prince.

"My muffins will be sweeter!"
said the princess.

"My cake will be even sweeter!"
said the queen.

"My pie will be the sweetest!"
said the king.

"My cookies are sweet!"
said the prince.

"My muffins are sweeter!"
said the princess.

"My cake is even sweeter!"
said the queen.

"My pie is... Hey! Where is my pie?"
asked the king.

"Your pie is almost ready, King," said the baker.

"What is taking so long?" asked the king. "I want my pie and I want it now!"

"King, your special pie is ready now!" said the baker.

"At last!" said the king. "Thank you! My pie is the sweetest! You will all soon see how sweet it is!"

"What makes that pie so sweet?" asked the prince and princess.

"Tell them, dear!" said the queen.

"My pie has 24 blackbirds singing tweet, tweet, tweet!"